Kenneth Grahame's

THE WIND IN THE WILLOWS

The Adventures of Mole, Rat, and Toad

Adapted by Janet Palazzo-Craig

Illustrated by Mary Alice Baer

TROLL ASSOCIATES

Library of Congress Cataloging in Publication Data

Palazzo-Craig, Janet.
    The adventures of Mole, Rat, and Toad.

    (Kenneth Grahame's The wind in the willows; 1)
    Adaptation of: The wind in the willows/Kenneth
Grahame.
    Summary: Mole and Rat visit Toad and are persuaded by
the latter to join him on a trip through the countryside
in a gypsy wagon.
    [1. Friendship—Fiction. 2. Animals—Fiction]
I. Baer, Mary Alice, ill. II. Grahame, Kenneth, 1859-
1932. Wind in the willows. III. Title. IV. Series:
Palazzo-Craig, Janet. Kenneth Grahame's The wind in the
willows; 1.
PZ7.P1762Af   [Fic]   81-16422
ISBN 0-89375-636-9   AACR2
ISBN 0-89375-637-7 (pbk.)

Printed in the United States of America
10 9 8 7 6 5 4 3 2

The Mole had been up very early, spring-cleaning his little home. Mopping and dusting, scouring and scrubbing, he worked and worked. His arms ached, and his black fur was tousled and full of dust. Suddenly, he threw down his mop and said, "Oh, hang spring-cleaning!" For even in his dark house, deep within the earth, spring had found the Mole.

In an instant, he was busily scraping his way along the tunnel that led to the sun and air. At last, his nose popped through the earth into the sunlight. Happily, the Mole began rolling in the grass of a great meadow. "This is the life!" he said. "Much better than mopping floors!"

The Mole crossed the meadow until he reached a hedge. An old rabbit sat nearby and told him, "You must pay to cross the hedge."

"Onion-sauce to you!" cried the Mole, and quickly, he pushed past the rabbit. It all happened so fast, the old rabbit just stood there sputtering. Soon the other rabbits were out, saying "Well, I would have said—" and "Why didn't you tell him—" But, of course, it was too late by then.

By this time, the Mole was far away. He watched the birds building nests and listened to their chirping. All around him, flowers were budding, and the leaves on the trees were about to unfold. Suddenly, he found himself at the edge of a river. The Mole was bewitched. He had never seen a river before. He watched the water dance and sparkle, as it bubbled on its way.

As he sat down, the Mole noticed the river bank across from him. A small, round face appeared. The face had small, neat ears and thick silky hair. There was a twinkle in his eyes. It was the Water Rat.

The two strangers looked at one another.

"Hello, Mole!" said the Water Rat.

"Hello, Rat!" said the Mole.

"Would you like to come over?" asked the Rat.

"Oh, it's all very well to *talk*—" said the Mole. He was a bit annoyed by the question, because he didn't see how he could possibly cross the river.

"Just wait," said the Rat. He jumped down the river bank and untied a small boat that was just the right size for two. Mole loved the boat at once, even though he didn't fully know what it was for. The Rat rowed across and helped his new friend into the boat.

"Look," said the Rat, "if you're not busy this morning, why don't we go for a row and a picnic? The lunch basket is packed and ready to go."

"Let's start at once," answered the Mole. "What a day I'm having," he said happily. "Here I am sitting in a boat—I've never been in one before, you know."

"Well, what *have* you been doing, then?" cried the Rat.

"Is rowing a boat really so nice?" asked the Mole shyly.

"Nice? Why it's the best there is. And let me tell you, life on the river can't be beat. It's my world, and I don't want any other." As the Rat rowed, the Mole sat back in the boat, trailing one paw in the water and daydreaming.

It wasn't long before the Mole realized he was very hungry from all his spring-cleaning and adventuring. They pulled the boat to shore and feasted on all the good things in the Rat's big lunch basket. After a while, the Rat said, "Well, I suppose we should start for home."

The afternoon sun was low in the sky as the Rat rowed gently along. He was in a dreamy mood and not paying much attention to Mole. But the Mole was full of lunch and had the feeling that he could do just about anything. It wasn't long before he said, "Ratty! Please, *I* want to row now!"

"Not yet, my friend," said the Rat. "Wait until you've had a
lesson." But more and more the Mole was feeling that he could
row every bit as well as the Rat. He jumped up and grabbed the
oars. Taken by surprise, the Rat fell backwards from his seat.
His legs kicked in the air. "Stop it, you silly animal!" he cried.
"You'll tip us over."

But it was too late. For Mole, swinging the oars with pride, missed the water completely, and lost his balance. *Sploosh!* The boat tipped. Oh, how cold the water felt, as the Mole sank down. Suddenly, a strong paw grabbed him by the neck. It was the Rat. He pulled the Mole to shore and swam back to get the boat and the picnic basket.

14

When they were ready to set off once again, a very sad and soaking-wet Mole said, "Ratty, I'm so sorry for what I've done. When I think how I might have lost your beautiful lunch basket! Can you ever forgive me?"

"That's all right," said the Rat. "What's a little wet to a Water Rat? But listen, why don't you come and stay with me for a while? My home is plain, but you'll be comfortable. And I'll teach you how to row and swim."

The Mole thought the Rat was very kind. Soon he was feeling rather good again. He even told off a couple of ducks, who had the bad manners to snicker at his untidy appearance.

At Rat's house, they lit a bright fire in the living room. As they sat in armchairs, the Rat told the Mole stories about life on the river. Each one was more exciting than the last. But soon, a very sleepy Mole had to be taken to his bedroom. As he fell asleep, he listened to the river murmuring softly outside his window.

This was only the first of many happy days for the Mole. He quickly learned to swim and row. Together, he and the Rat would travel up and down the river, calling to their friends on the river banks. Sometimes they would stop their rowing, and listen to the wind whispering among the reeds and willows.

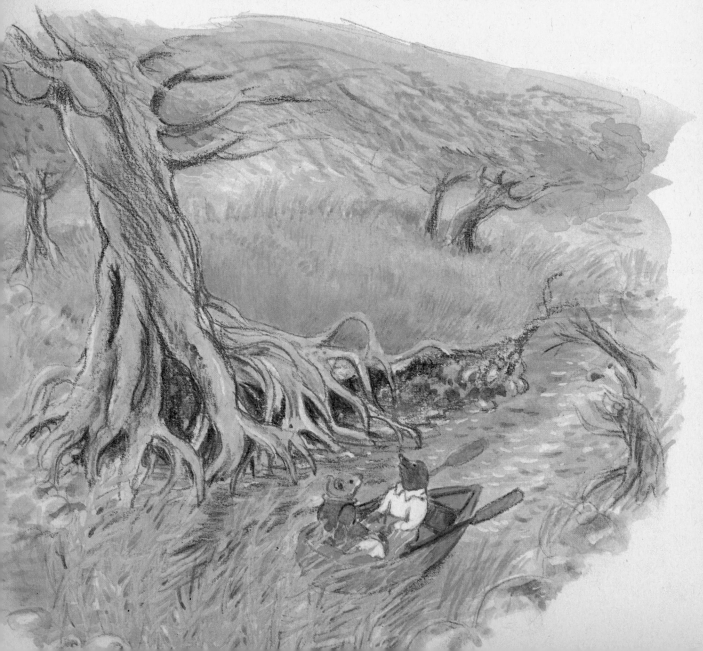

One summer morning, the Rat was busily scribbling a song he'd written about his friends, the ducks. He was very much impressed with it and kept singing it over and over. "Excuse me, Ratty," said the Mole politely. "I wonder if we could visit Mr. Toad—you've told me so much about him."

"Why, of course," said the good-natured Rat. "We'll get out the boat and go right now! Toad is always happy to see his friends."

"He must be a very good animal," said the Mole.

"Yes, he is," replied the Rat. "Perhaps he is a bit boastful—and somewhat conceited. But, after all, nobody's perfect."

Rounding a bend in the river, they saw a beautiful, old brick house, with neat green lawns reaching down to the water's edge. It was Toad Hall. They left the boat and walked through gardens of colorful flowers. Toad was sitting in a wicker chair, with a large map spread before him. When he saw Mole and Rat, he jumped up and danced around them in excitement. "You're just the two I wanted to see!" he cried, without even waiting for an introduction to the Mole.

They settled into lawn chairs, and the Mole remarked how much he liked Toad Hall. "Finest house on the river," agreed the Toad boastfully. The Rat nudged the Mole, as if to say "I told you so." But by this time, the Toad was saying, "What good luck that you're here. Let me show you something." He led them to the stable, and there they saw a gypsy wagon, painted bright yellow, with green and red wheels.

"There it is!" Toad said proudly. "We'll take this cart on the open road—through villages, towns, and countryside. Travel and excitement—it's the only way to live!" He took them inside the wagon, and it really was very comfortable. The shelves were lined with books and cans of food; there were little bunk beds, a stove for cooking, and plenty of pots and pans.

"Everything's here," said the Toad. "You'll find nothing has been forgotten, when we make our start this afternoon."

At this, the Rat looked up, saying, "Did I hear you say something about 'we' and 'our start' and 'this afternoon'?"

"Now Ratty," said the Toad, "you've both got to come with me."

"I'm not going, and that's final!"

The Mole was a little disappointed, for he had fallen in love with the yellow wagon. But like a loyal friend, he agreed with the Rat.

"Well, come and have some lunch," said the Toad, "and we'll talk about it."

Somehow, by the end of the meal, Toad and Mole were planning all the wonderful things they would do and see on the open road. The Rat hated to disappoint the Mole, so at last he agreed.

They got the cart ready and rounded up Toad's old gray horse, who wasn't the least bit happy to begin the journey. At last, they set off. Birds called and whistled to them cheerfully, as they passed along a dusty road. Other travelers waved or stopped to say nice things about their wagon. Late that evening, tired and happy and miles from home, they ate their supper and turned into their bunks.

After so much fresh air, the Toad slept very soundly. In fact, Rat and Mole couldn't get him out of bed the next morning. They began the day's work, making breakfast, cleaning dishes, and getting ready to start out again. Everything was done when Toad appeared, saying what a pleasant, easy life they were all leading now.

They had a good ride that day, and that afternoon they reached a wide road. They were rolling along easily, when far behind them they heard a low hum. Looking back, they saw a cloud of dust speeding toward them. With a blast of wind and a whirl of sound, it was on them! *Poop-poop*! it wailed. They jumped for the nearest ditch, and the cart went rolling out of control and toppled—a complete wreck. For an instant, they saw what it was—a beautiful car, it's paint and metal shining brightly. Then it was gone.

The Rat jumped into the road, shaking his fist at the car and shouting many impolite things. Meanwhile, the Mole tried to calm the old horse. But where was Toad? There he sat in the middle of the road, as if in a trance. Every so often he would smile and say, *"Poop-poop!"*

"Aren't you going to help us with the cart?" called the Rat.

"The cart?" answered Toad. "I hope I never see the cart again. Now I've discovered the only way to travel! What a glorious sight! What dust clouds I shall raise as I speed along! What a great future lies before me!" He went on like this all the way home, which was quite a long way.

The Mole and the Rat were very tired when they finally reached the snug comfort of Rat's little house. But after a bit of supper, they felt much better. How glad they were to be back on the river bank! They talked and laughed about Toad and the adventures they had shared on the open road.

The next afternoon, as Mole sat on the bank fishing, along came the Rat. "Heard the news?" he asked the Mole. "Toad went to town this morning, and he's bought himself a fancy motor-car!" The two just shook their heads and laughed, promising one another that *they* wouldn't be Toad's passengers ever again!

Or would they?

Poop-poop!